1 It fell upon a summer day

words: St...
music: H...
Someone's sin...

It — fell u-pon — a — sum - mer day, when Je - sus walked in Ga - li - lee, The

mo - thers from a vil - lage brought their chil - dren to his — knee.

2 It's me O Lord

spiritual
Alleluya 51

descant 1

descant 2

treble or tenor

It's me, it's me, it's me O Lord, standing in the need of prayer, It's

Fine

me, it's me, it's me O Lord, standing in the need of prayer.

3 Amazing grace

words : John Newton
music : traditional
Ta-ra-ra boom-de-ay 28 (in F)

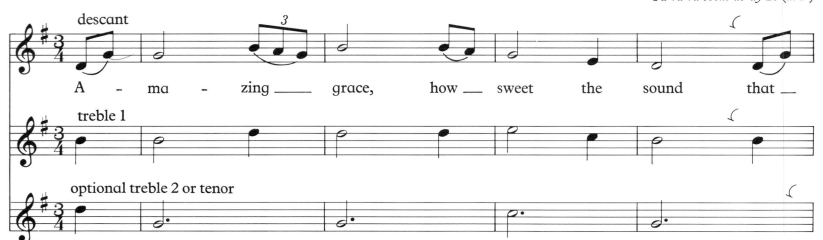

descant

A - ma - zing ___ grace, how ___ sweet the sound that ___

treble 1

optional treble 2 or tenor

saved a ___ wretch like ___ me. _____ I ___ once was ___

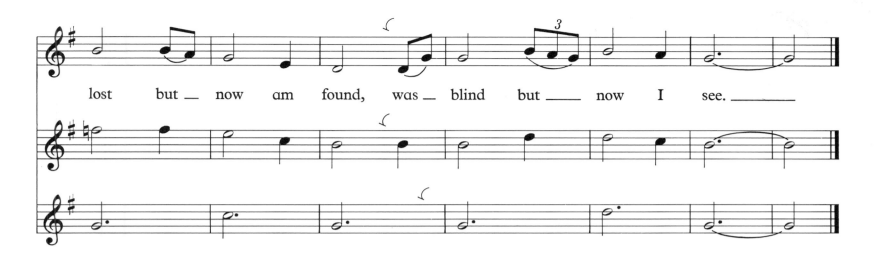

lost but — now am found, was — blind but ___ now I see. _____

4 Michael, row the boat ashore

spiritual
Ta-ra-ra boom-de-ay 30

descant

Mi-chael, row the boat a-shore, Hal-le-lu - jah, Mi-chael

tenor

row the boat a-shore, Hal-le-lu - jah.

5 Yellow submarine

John Lennon/Paul McCartney
Apusskidu 4 (in F)

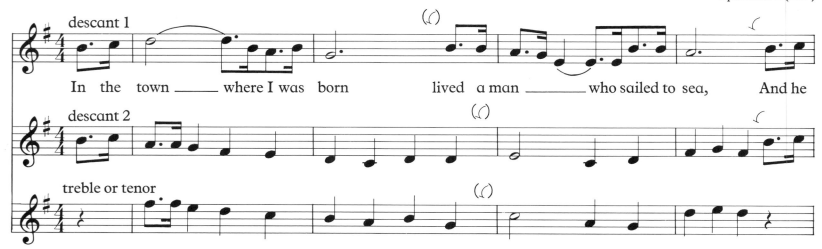

In the town ____ where I was born   lived a man ____ who sailed to sea,   And he

told ____ us of his life   in the land ____ of submarines.

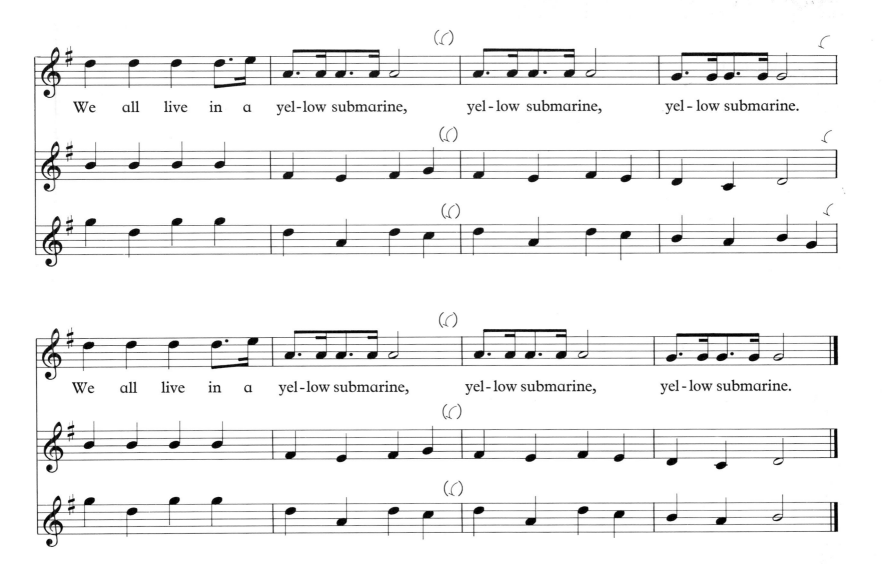

We all live in a yel-low submarine, yel-low submarine, yel-low submarine.

We all live in a yel-low submarine, yel-low submarine, yel-low submarine.

6 Morning has broken

words: Eleanor Farjeon
music: traditional
Someone's singing Lord 3

descant 1

Morn – ing has bro – ken like the first morn – ing.

descant 2

(or) treble or tenor 1

tenor 2

Black – bird has spo – ken like the first bird. _____

Praise for the sing - ing! Praise for the morn - ing!

Praise for them, spring - ing fresh from the Lord.

7 Short'nin' bread

American plantation song, arr. Wolfe/Wood
Ta-ra-ra boom-de-ay 43

descant 1

Three lit - tle child - ren ly-ing in bed, two were sick and the o -ther 'most dead.

descant 2

treble or tenor 1

tenor 2 (optional)

Sent for the doc - tor, the doc - tor said "Feed those child-ren on short -nin' bread".

Mammy's lit-tle ba-by loves short-nin', short-nin', Mammy's lit-tle ba-by loves short-nin' bread.

Mammy's lit-tle ba-by loves short-nin', short-nin', Mammy's lit-tle ba-by loves short-nin' bread.

The descant 2 part, re-written an octave higher, could be played on treble.

8 When a knight won his spurs

words: Jan Struther
music: traditional hymn tune
Someone's Singing Lord 34

descant 1

descant 2

(or) treble 1

treble 2 or tenor

When a knight won his spurs, in the sto - ries of old, he was gen - tle and

brave, he was gal - lant and bold, With a shield on his arm and a

lance in his hand for __ God and for va - lour he rode through the land.

9 Silent night

words: *Joseph Mohr*
music: *Franz Grüber*

descant 1

descant 2

(or) treble

tenor

Si – lent night, ho – ly night. All is calm, all is bright,

Round yon Vir – gin Mo-ther and Child. Ho – ly In -fant so ten - der and mild,

Sleep   in hea – ven – ly   peace, _____   sleep ___ in hea – ven – ly   peace!

10 Day oh

traditional Jamaican
Mango Spice 27 (in D)

descant 1

1st time 2nd time

Day oh, day — oh, — day-light come an me wan go home, wan go home.

descant 2

(or) treble 1

treble 2 or tenor

1st time 2nd time

Come Missa Tallyman, tal-ly ba-na-na, Daylight come an me wan go home, wan go home.

Six han, seven han, eight han bunch, Daylight come an me wan go home, wan go home.

Day oh, day oh, daylight come an me wan go home, wan go home.

11 Procession

Graham Westcott

12 You are my sunshine

Jimmy Davis/Carl Mitchell
Ta-ra-ra boom-de-ay 16

descant

You are my sun-shine, _____ my on-ly sun-shine, _____ you make me

treble

hap-py _____ when skies are grey. _____ You'll ne-ver know, dear, _____ how much I

love you. _____ Please don't take my sun-shine a - way. _____

13 Dance of the cuckoos

Marvin Hatley

TURN OVER

The descant 2 part, re-written an octave higher, could be played on treble.

14 Dis long time, gal

traditional Jamaican
Mango Spice 32

descant

Dis   long time, gal, me never   see   you,   Come mek me hol your han.   Dis

treble

bass xylophone

long   time, gal, me ne -ver   see   you,   Come mek me hol your   han.

Peel head John Crow sid u - pon tree - top, pick off de blos - som, mek me hol your

han, gal, mek me hol your han. Mek me wheel an

turn till we tum - ble dung, mek me hol your han, gal. han, gal.

coda

1st time 2nd time

15 Where have all the flowers gone?

Pete Seeger
Alleluya 37

flowing and lyrical

Where have all the flowers gone? Long time passing. Where have all the flowers gone? Long time a - go.

Where have all   the   flowers   gone ?   Girls have picked them ev – 'ry   one.   When will they

e -ver learn ?   When will they   e   –   ver   learn ? _____   learn ?

1st time   2nd time

16 What have they done to the rain?

Malvina Reynolds
Alleluya 35

rain? _____ Just a lit-tle boy standing in the rain, the gen-tle rain that

falls for years, _____ And the grass is gone, the boy dis-ap-pears, and rain keeps

fal-ling like help-less tears, and what have they done to the rain? _____

17 Bourrée

Bach
from Suite in A minor

descant 1

descant 2 or tenor

Acknowledgements

We are most grateful to all the teachers and advisers who have helped us to prepare this book. Our particular thanks to Bob Mason, Martin Sheldon and Cynthia Watson.

The following copyright owners have kindly granted their permission for the reprinting of words and music:

Boosey & Hawkes Music Publishers Ltd, Allans Music Australia Pty Ltd and Harold Flammer Inc for 7 'Short'nin' bread', © 1928 Harold Flammer Inc, Delaware Water Gap, PA 18327.

Harmony Music Ltd for 15 'Where have all the flowers gone', used by permission of Harmony Music Ltd. Also by permission of the Canadian publishers, Fall River Music Inc, © 1961 by Fall River Music Inc. All rights reserved. Used by permission.

David Higham Associates Ltd for the words of 6 'Morning has broken'.

Robert Kingston (Music) Ltd for Eastern Hemisphere and Hatley Music Company USA, Western Hemisphere, for 13 'Dance of the cuckoos', © Hatley Music Company, USA.

Northern Songs Ltd for 5 'Yellow submarine', © 1966 by Northern Songs Ltd. Used by permission of Music Sales Ltd, 8-9 Frith Street, London W1V 5TZ.

Oxford University Press for the words of 8 'When a knight won his spurs'.

Peermusic (UK) Ltd, 8-14 Verulam Street, London WC1X 8LZ and Allans Music Australia Pty Ltd for 12 'You are my sunshine', © Peer International Corp, USA.

TRO Essex Music Ltd and Schroder Music Co for 16 'What have they done to the rain', © 1962 Schroder Music Co. Reproduced by permission of TRO Essex Music Ltd.

Graham Westcott for 11 'Procession'.

First published 1982 by A & C Black (Publishers) Ltd, 35 Bedford Row, London WC1R 4JH.
© 1982 A & C Black (Publishers) Ltd
Reprinted 1982 (twice), 1984, 1985, 1987, 1991, 1993.

ISBN: 0-7136-2167-2

Printed by Caligraving Limited, Thetford, Norfolk